KATHA

First reprint 2010
Copyright © Katha, 2006
First Published by Katha in KPS 2, 1992
Copyright © for the story in its original
language is held by the author.

Copyright © for the English
translation rests with KATHA.

ISBN 978-81-89020-68-2

KATHA
A-3 Sarvodaya Enclave
Sri Aurobindo Marg, New Delhi 110 017
Phone: 2652 4350, 2652 4511
Fax: 2651 4373

E-mail: kathakaar@katha.org
Website: www.katha.org

For orders and enquiries, contact Katha marketing and sales division,
A-3 Sarvodaya Enclave, Sri Aurobindo Marg, New Delhi 110 017

# Satyadas

*an amazing mystery by*
BIMAL KAR

*exploring truth, falsehood and everything in between*

translated from the Bangla by Enakshi Chatterjee
art by Neeta Gangopadhya

Rain, rain, rain. For five long dreary days and nights, the rain poured down on Nishipur. Raghunath was bored. Business had never been so slow.

Raghunath owned a grocery shop. It stood in a quiet lane at the very edge of this small mining town in Bengal. The shop was fairly well stocked. There was rice, pulses, salt, cooking oil, onions, potatoes, muri and batasa. Still, the takings were scarcely enough to scrape by.

Raghunath hoped that things would change. He did not expect to do as well as the Haladhars. They ran the oldest grocery store in the neighbourhood. Their shop sold everything from tinned milk to mosquito nets. But he could not understand why his sales were lower than some of the other small shops. He was polite to his customers. His goods were never overpriced. He never tried to palm off stale stuff. As it was, he barely made enough money. He had to support himself and his wife Yamuna, and pay young Bishu's wages. Bishu was lame. He had been hired to do odd jobs around the shop. Raghunath often ended up doing most of the work himself.

Darkness was already falling. Raghunath sat watching the rain drip onto the shrubbery outside his shop. The crows huddled under the branches of the trees, trying to stay dry. The waterlogged lane was deserted.

"You had better go home," he said to Bishu. "Don't get drenched, you'll catch a chill. Cover your head."

Bishu wrapped a sheet of torn polythene around his head and set off into the gloom.

It was almost closing time. Raghunath was about to begin his evening prayers. Suddenly a movement in the shadows outside caught his eye. He stopped to look. A man stepped out of the grey drizzle. A stranger. Hair unkempt, chin unshaven, he carried a black faded umbrella in one hand and a wooden box in the other. From his right shoulder hung a cloth bundle. He wore a grimy dhoti. The frayed black coat over his shirt had some buttons missing. It had been mended in several places. His slippers were worn out.

"What do you want?" asked Raghunath.

The stranger put down his box. "Can I get some puffed rice here, babu?" he asked.

Raghunath nodded. "But it won't be good. Muri tends to get soggy in this weather."

"Well then, some chira and gur will do."

The man set down his belongings on the rickety old bench.

"Where are you from?" asked Raghunath.

"Dharmapur."

Raghunath had never heard of the place. There were several other mining towns within ten miles of Nishipur. Perhaps Dharmapur was one of them.

"Babu, I would like to wash my hands. May I have some water in a lota?"

Raghunath was wary of letting a stranger in. He fetched a bucket of water and a tin mug. "Go on, wash up. The water is from my well."

Embarrassed, the man said, "Why babu, a small lota of water would have done."

"You are covered in mud. Go ahead. Have a wash."

The man moved a little away and began to clean up.

"What is your name?" asked Raghunath.

"You can call me Satyadas."

He finished washing his feet. Then he rinsed his mouth, and said, "Nice water you have here, babu. Tastes good."

"Where are you off to in this rain?"

"Can't say for sure. I just set out, wherever my legs take me ..."

Raghunath smiled. "But you need to stop for the night."

"Well yes. But then, any shelter will do," Satyadas gave back the bucket and mug.

"Just a minute," Raghunath said.

"You need a dish to soak your chira and gur?"

"I have a bowl."

Satyadas made to untie his bundle.

"Don't bother to open that. I'll get you one," said Raghunath.

He came back with an enamelled dish and water in a lota. "Here. Soak the stuff in this. You can wash it after you have eaten."

The man seemed famished. It was only rice flakes and jaggery. Still, he wolfed it down.

"What do you do for a living, Satyadas?"

A smile flitted across his face. "I roam about, selling herbal cures, roots and things."

"Roots and things?"

"Herbs to cure scorpion bites, snakebites, old wounds, indigestion, rheumatic pain ..."

"Are they any good for snakebite? I have seen a few cases. The roots are no good."

"Snake venom is of different kinds, babu. These herbal cures are no good if the snake is very poisonous. But they work for the less deadly ones."

"Did you say you had something for rheumatic pain? My wife suffers from rheumatism ..."

"Yes, I have something for that. Not for old pain though. What I have is good for recent attacks. Like the aches that flare up during the rains."

Satyadas had another drink of water. He went out and washed the vessels. The dish and lota were put away.

"Who waits for you at home?" Raghunath asked.

"Nobody. I am a wanderer. God is with me." Satyadas smiled to himself.

Raghunath eyed him.

A vagabond, he thought.

It was time to pull down the shutters. But where would Satyadas go? The rain was coming down hard.

Raghunath did not know what to do. He could not send him out in this weather. Nor could he keep him company until it cleared up.

"Satyadas, it is raining again. You can't leave. You had better wait here. I have to go in. It is time for my evening puja."

Satyadas jumped up. "Oh no, no! I am keeping you from your prayers. I'm so sorry. I shall leave ..."

"Where will you go in this rain? Stay a while. Leave when the rain stops. I will be inside. Call out before you go."

"Then let me pay you right now, babu."

Raghunath felt a little ashamed. Accept money from this penniless vagabond? For such a small thing? The poor man had strayed in here in bad weather. He had eaten some chira. It wasn't worth more than a rupee perhaps. Raghunath would not be poorer for the loss of a rupee.

"Forget it. You don't need to pay."

Satyadas stared at him. "No babu, I cannot allow that."

"Why not?"

"I may be illiterate, but you have read the Shastras, the old holy books. It is against dharma not to pay, they say."

"Enough of your dharma!" Raghunath said. With a brief smile, he added, "All right. You win. Give me fifty paisa."

"That is too little, babu."

"It's all I want. I shall follow my dharma. You keep yours."

Satyadas fumbled in his pocket for a coin. Then, an idea seemed to strike him. And he began to undo the rope tied around his box instead.

"Pay me later," Raghunath said. "There's no hurry."

"No babu, please …"

Satyadas by now had opened the box. There were some very strange things inside: tiny paper packets, glass bowls, a pair of tumblers, small black balls, the size of jamuns, a stick, some coloured handkerchiefs. He rummaged about a bit and pulled out a black cloth pouch.

As Satyadas opened the pouch, something fell out.

A gold coin! Satyadas didn't notice, but Raghunath did. Where did this poor peddler get hold of a gold coin?

"Here you are, babu." Satyadas offered him the money. "You could have taken a rupee at least."

Raghunath, still stunned, only said, "No. Fifty paisa will do."

He took the money. Then he looked at the box and said, trying to sound as casual as possible, "Quite a collection you have here!"

"Well, this is my magic box."

"Magic box?"

"I wander around quite a bit. I have to sell my wares. I attract customers with magic – card tricks, sleight of hand, a little juggling. I can turn water into different colours. You have to do all sorts of things to earn a living."

"So you are a magician as well!" Raghunath laughed. "You are a man of many talents, Satyadas."

Satyadas looked embarrassed. "Oh no sir! I am a poor man. A nobody."

"If you say so. You stay right here. I'm going in. Just let me know when you leave."

Raghunath lowered the shutters a little before he went in.

When Raghunath came out after his evening puja, the rain had stopped. Satyadas sat hunched up on the bench. A ragged sheet was thrown over him. The box was on the floor. A sling bag, from which the sheet had been taken, lay half open beside it. He was shivering.

"Satyadas —

can you hear me?"

Satyadas pushed the sheet off his face,
"Yes babu?"

"What's wrong?"

"Fever. I've had it for the last three years. It comes and goes.
Don't you worry sir. I'll be fine. I'll leave as soon as the fever
comes down."

Slightly offended, Raghunath said, "Who is asking you to leave?
It is the fever I'm worried about. You're shivering so."

"It comes on from all this walking in the rain, babu. But it
will go."

"Even if the fever goes, stay here tonight. You can sleep in
the shop."

"But that's impossible! A sick man in your house?"

"Do as I say. I'm going in now. I'll come back later."

Raghunath pulled the shutter down a little further. He moved
the small lantern to a corner of the room.

Raghunath sat in the back room. He was reciting from the Ramayana. His voice was singsong. Yamuna's needle flew across a piece of kantha embroidery. They heard a sound from the shop.

"He must be up," Yamuna said. "Why don't you go and have a look?"

Raghunath stood up. "Something's fishy about that fellow. Makes a living selling roots and potions. Where did that gold coin come from?"

"Could be brass for all we know."

"No. It is pure gold," Raghunath insisted. "My father worked in a goldsmith's shop. I have seen plenty of the stuff."

"And a fat lot of good it's done you. Did it bring you good luck? All we've done is move up from one room to two. You have the luck of tin. Certainly not gold – not even brass!"

"What I can't understand is how that beggar came by the gold coin."

"Perhaps he inherited it."

"But he has nobody in this world."

"I hope he's not a thief."

Raghunath shook his head. "He seems like an honest man. Besides he is our guest. We must not speak ill of our guests."

"All right. But why don't you go and see what he's up to?"

Putting the Ramayana aside, Raghunath went into the shop. He found Satyadas sitting up, wiping the perspiration from his forehead and neck. He smiled.

"My fever's come down, babu."

"All the same, stay the night," Raghunath said. He pointed to the shutter. "Shall I close it fully? We'll have to shut the back door. Is that all right with you?"

Suddenly Satyadas blurted out, "You are a very kind man, babu. A good man. Nobody lets a stranger into their home. You have given me shelter. The All Seeing One misses nothing. Isn't that true?"

Raghunath shrugged. "So He does. That is why I'm in such a wretched state. I sold my land to set up shop here. Everything grows with time. But in my case nothing has. I started with a single shed. After seven years of hard work, all I have to show for my pains is two sheds. That's all. The All Seeing One has seen nothing. He seems to have a stiff neck. If he looks eastwards, he can't turn west."

Satyadas stared at his host with unblinking eyes. A strange smile lit up his face.

Unwilling to continue the conversation, Raghunath said, "You can have some chapatti and vegetables if you are hungry."

Satyadas nodded. He sat very, very still.

Next morning, the sky was clear. Soon bright sunshine flooded the earth. Satyadas had a wash by the well. He made a polite namaste to Yamuna, who was sweeping the yard. When he was done, he went in to tie up his bundle and pack his box. Raghunath stopped him just as he was about to leave. "You can't go on an empty stomach. Tea's coming."

"What a good idea. I'm rather fond of tea."

"Where will you go from here?"

"Wherever my legs take me."

Yamuna brought the tea.

"Here, take this. Let me get you a biscuit," Raghunath said, handing him the cup. He fetched some homemade biscuits.

"It's a beautiful day, babu. The Sun God smiles on us. The earth is clean and fresh."

The new day had brought hope to Raghunath as well. The crows were up and about. Sparrows chirruped in the bushes. A dog loitered in front of the shop.

Satyadas washed his cup and handed it back. "I must go, babu."

"So long then."

"I'm just a crazy beggar. You were kind enough to give me food and shelter. Nobody does these days. May God bless you."

"How long before you pass this way again?"

"Maybe a week, maybe a couple of months."

"Don't forget to look us up if you come this way."

"Most certainly, babu." Satyadas folded his hands in a namaste. Then off he went.

Raghunath watched him go.

The day started off in right earnest. Bishu came. Raghunath bustled in and out of the shop, barking orders.

Bishu knew the order of his daily tasks. First he must sweep the shop floor. Then his master would sprinkle water on the doorway. He would light the agarbatti and bow reverently to the picture of Lakshmi. He would put some rice and turmeric on a plate, and the day's business would begin.

Raghunath stood outside while Bishu swept the floor. Somewhere a crow cawed. Someone was sawing wood.

Suddenly Bishu's excited shout broke the morning peace. "Babu, babu – look at this."

He picked up something from the floor. Raghunath recognized it instantly. It was the black cloth pouch from which Satyadas had taken the money.

He weighed it in his hand. It felt heavy. How could Satyadas forget his most precious possession? He did not carry much money on him. He'd be sure to get into trouble. He would have to come all the way back for it.

Raghunath paused. He had seen a gold coin fall from this very pouch. Satyadas must have discovered it by now. It must be in the box.

Unless ...

He felt a tightness in his chest. His breathing grew shallow. He was strangely reluctant to look into the pouch. He glanced at Bishu. The boy was busy. Raghunath pulled the strings apart and picked out a coin. He was the son of a goldsmith. He knew. These were gold coins all right. Fairly old – perhaps from the Queen's time.

He turned and went in.

"Yamuna, can you come here a minute?"

Yamuna was by the well, hanging out the washing.

"What is it?"

Raghunath held out his palm. "Gold. That man left it behind."

"Gold?" Yamuna froze. She crept forward to get a closer look. Yamuna had never seen a gold coin before. "Show me, show me," she said, all excited.

Raghunath gave her the coin. Yamuna fingered it lovingly. She may never have handled a gold coin before, but she certainly knew what gold was when she saw it.

"How many?"

"Six!"

"Six?"

"Six gold coins and two rings."

Yamuna stared at her husband. "Shut the door," she said. "Bishu can walk in at any minute."

"I just don't understand," Raghunath muttered. "These are old coins, embossed with the Queen's portrait. How did he get hold of them?"

"What are those stones in the rings?"

"I don't know much about stones.
One is dark and the other is light, almost transparent. They look like precious stones."

"A diamond?"

Raghunath picked up one of the rings and held it up to the light.

"Could be," he said, sounding cleverer than he felt.

"And the other one?"

He brought out the other ring. It was set with a dark stone. "I don't know ... could be a sapphire ..."

Raghunath swept everything back into the pouch.

"Who is this Satyadas?" he wondered aloud. "He certainly didn't look like the sort of person to be walking about with a pouch full of gold and jewellery. Why, he couldn't even scrape together five rupees. Where did these six gold coins and two rings come from?"

"Perhaps he stole them," Yamuna decided. "Perhaps he lost his nerve and fled."

Raghunath shook his head. Satyadas did not look like a thief. He looked more like a peddler who did magic tricks for his customers.

"Satyadas is a magician you know. He told me so."

"Ah! that explains it," said Yamuna. "They're props. Fake gold and gems for his bag of tricks."

But Raghunath was not convinced.

"What will you do?" Yamuna asked.

"Let me see ..." Raghunath scratched his head. "Surely he will miss the pouch. He will come back for it. After all it isn't just a couple of rupees."

Bishu was calling to them.

Yamuna whispered, "So what do we do now?"

"Slip the pouch into your trunk when no one is looking. Don't breathe a word about it to anybody. Be very careful. Times are bad. Can't trust a soul these days"

# more than equal footing

Satyadas did not return the next day. Or the day after.

A week went by. Raghunath expected him to turn up any minute. All day, even in the dead of night, he waited. While he was attending to his customers, he waited. He never took his eyes off the road. Satyadas might at any moment appear through the trees – bag slung over his shoulder, box in one hand, legs covered with dust.

Weeks passed into months. The winter winds blew the leaves off the trees and turned the grass brown.

Had he been arrested? Raghunath wondered. Perhaps the coins were stolen. But Satyadas did not look like a crook.

"Do you think he's dead?" Raghunath asked his wife.

"He's not coming back, that's for sure."

Raghunath waited. Perhaps Satyadas might come for the Vaishakhi fair. All sorts of people came. But Vaishakhi came and went. There was still no sign of Satyadas.

A year passed. The monsoons came again. But no Satyadas.

Then one day, Raghunath decided to sell a gold coin. Times were hard. They couldn't wait forever. He went into town and sold one coin to Chandu the goldsmith. He bought a sari for Yamuna.

On the way home, he bought some things for the house.

That night Raghunath and Yamuna talked for a long time. What should they fix up first – the house or the shop? They decided to buy more supplies for the shop.

Of course the money did not last long. Yamuna suggested they sell another coin.

"But I can't go to Chandu babu again," Raghunath protested. "I lied to him. He might get suspicious. Where would poor people like us find one gold coin after another?"

"What will you do?"

"I know the going rate now. Nobody can cheat me. I'd better go to Burdwan. I'll take the morning train and be back by evening."

Raghunath came back from Burdwan looking cheerful. "I got thirty more. The price of gold keeps going up."

Before the Pujas, Raghunath had spent three of the coins. He was enjoying himself. His shop had a new look. Now he had proper tin chairs, sturdy shutters, better stuff on sale. His home looked much more prosperous. People wondered at Raghunath the grocer's good fortune. He

made up a story.
The money, he said, had
come from Yamuna's uncle,
who had died recently, leaving
everything to his niece.

One day, Raghunath said to Yamuna, "Remember how people once looked down on me ... Look at them now. Haladhar babu's eldest son Sasadhar came to invite me to their Puja. You must come, he said. Father specially asked that you come."

"Hmmm …" Yamuna was pleased. So they were now equals with the rich Haladhars.

*satyadas*

The Pujas were over. Raghunath's shop was flourishing. They had hired one more boy. Business was brisk throughout the day.

Yamuna had almost everything she had ever wanted. The rooms had been repaired. They had covered the veranda. Her kitchen and store sparkled. She even had a proper bathroom.

Raghunath was a happy man.

Winter seemed to come early that year.

That evening, Raghunath was about to close the shop. He had just turned out the lights. Only a lantern burned in a corner, casting long shadows on the walls. Raghunath put his hand on the shutter to pull it down. Suddenly, he stopped short. A customer had stepped in.

"Wh … who is it?" Raghunath called nervously.

"Babu, it's me."

That voice! Raghunath froze, straining to get a better look at his shadowy visitor.

"Satyadas?"

"Namaskar babu."

He had the same weather weary look. He now had a straggly
beard. But the sling bag and wooden box were the same. The same
umbrella, the same black coat. The only addition was a coarse
muffler.

Satyadas put his luggage down.

"How have you been babu?"

Raghunath could not get any words out. It was as if a noose
was tightening around his neck. He just stood there and stared
blankly at the man in his shop. Was this really Satyadas?

"I was passing this way. I did promise to look you up."

Raghunath struggled to find his voice. "Where have you come from?" he croaked.

"Hridaypur. How are you? And the dear lady?"

Raghunath, still stunned, just nodded.

Satyadas looked around the shop. A small smile played on his lips.

"The last time I was here, it was pouring."

Raghunath eyed him suspiciously. Why was he here?

Satyadas coughed. He cleared his throat. "My throat is sore. May I have some tea? I still remember that steaming hot tea your wife made for me the last time."

Raghunath raised the wick of the lantern. "Have a seat," he said, remembering his manners.

In their room, Yamuna was massaging her chafed feet with cream and coconut oil. She wore a handloom sari with a coloured blouse. Her hair was neatly combed. These days she looked every bit the wife of a prosperous shopkeeper.

"He's here," Raghunath said tersely.

"Who?"

"Satyadas."

"Satyadas? Here?"

"Yes. Walked in a moment ago."

She stood up. "He's still alive?"

"So it seems."

"Did he ask for anything?"

"Not yet. He just walked in. Wants some tea. Has a cold, a sore throat." Raghunath made a feeble attempt to smile. "Says he hasn't forgotten the tea you made the last time."

Yamuna made a face.

"What shall we do with him?"

"Give him some tea first."

"Don't say anything," Yamuna warned. "Can you get rid of him?"

Raghunath shook his head. "He wants to spend the night here. Perhaps he'll leave tomorrow."

"Be careful. Don't give anything away. If he asks, deny everything."

She went in to make the tea.

Satyadas sipped his tea with relish stopping only to cough once in a while. Raghunath sat a couple of feet away. Satyadas said, "My chest is weak, babu. The slightest change in the weather sets me coughing."

"How about that fever?"

"It comes and goes. Won't leave me."

"And your herbals?"

"Same as always. Went all the way to Panchkot you know, for some special roots. There is one particular kind I wanted. But do you ever get what you want?"

Raghunath looked distracted. "So you spent the whole year travelling?"

"That is my fate. May I have a bidi please?"

"You shouldn't smoke with that cough."

"Just a few puffs," Satyadas said. "Then I'll have a wash. I'll spend the night here. I had a very comfortable stay the last time. You and the lady are so kind."

Raghunath could not hide his dismay. "Since you have come to stay the night, you must. But you will have to excuse me. I need to say my prayers ..." he said lamely.

"Yes, of course, babu."

Raghunath was in no mood to say his prayers. He sat on his bed, the Ramayana unopened in his lap. Yamuna stood close to him.

"Keep your mouth shut. Don't fall into a trap," she advised. "It isn't as if you stole the treasure from him. If people leave things behind, it's not your fault, is it? Finders keepers, they say."

"Well, I did wait. Month after month. What was I expected to do? He didn't turn up. After all I am human. How long could I leave the gold to rot in its pouch?"

"Why did he have to come back?" Yamuna grumbled.

"It is our bad luck."

"Why did he choose to come back now? He could have come earlier. The scoundrel! The crook!"

"Get him something to eat, quick. I don't want to talk to him," Raghunath said. "I hope he leaves first thing in the morning."

His meal over, Satyadas was getting ready for bed, when Raghunath went in again.

"Your shop looks very nice," Satyadas said by way of conversation.

Raghunath glanced warily at him. But Satyadas was rummaging in his bag for a sheet. His face was hidden.

He went on, "You have a lot of stuff here. It's like any other big store. Very nice. I like it babu."

Raghunath mumbled some feeble excuse. He was afraid of more awkward questions. But Satyadas only said, "Your house has been done up beautifully too. Well done, babu!"

Raghunath felt the ground slipping away from under his feet. He could not look Satyadas in the eye. He was uncomfortable, afraid.

"Have to go in. Had a hard day at the shop." He yawned.

"I am sorry babu, I should have realized. Please go ahead."

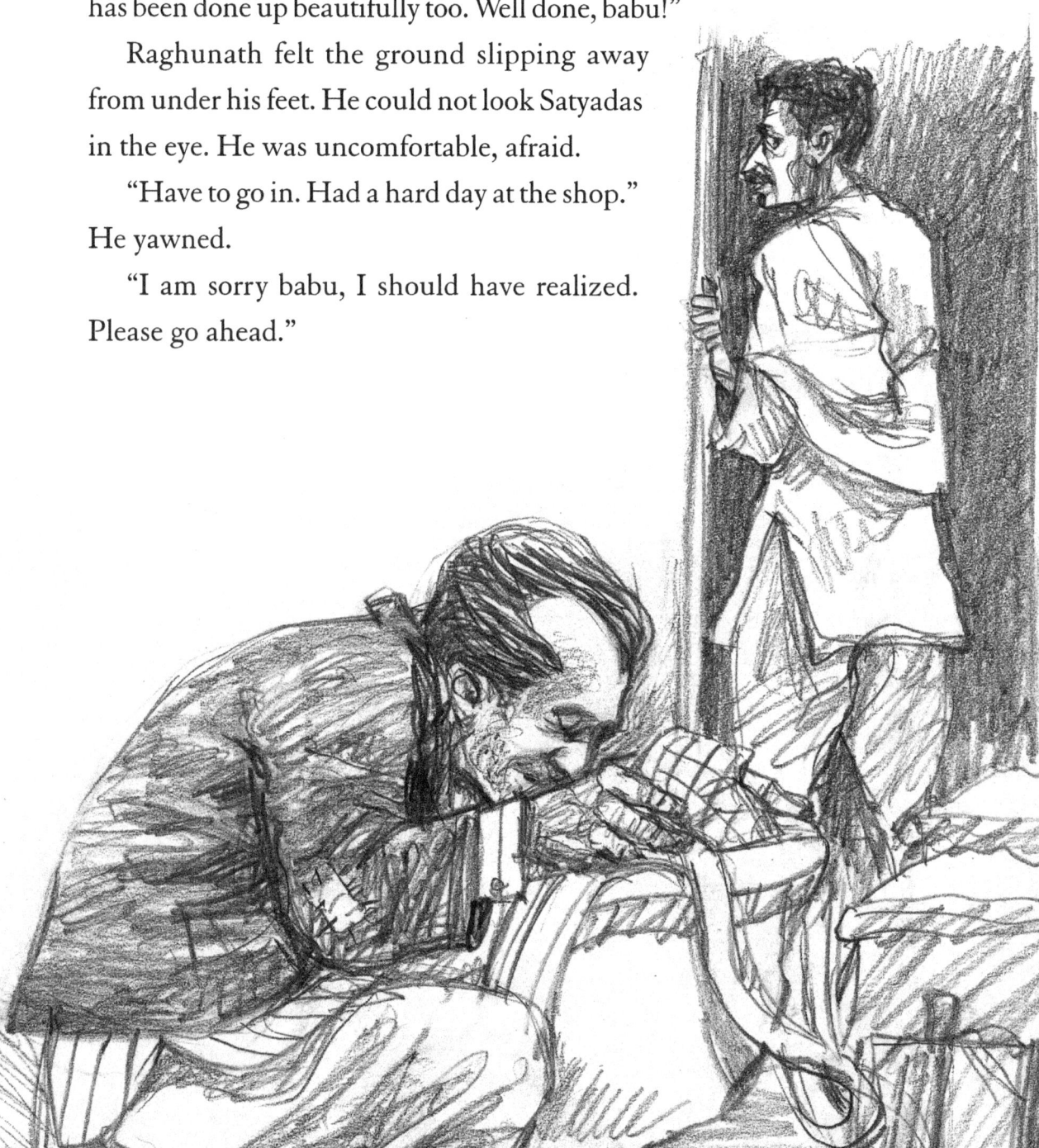

"Are you sure you have everything you need?"

"Of course. Nice place, very comfortable."

"Good night then. Are you …?"

"Yes, I will leave early in the morning tomorrow. There's a place I must get to by tomorrow. But I sleep like a log. Would you please wake me up in the morning?"

"Yes, certainly."

Later, Yamuna asked, "Did he mention the pouch?"

"No"

"That's odd."

Raghunath did not reply.

"Clearly the treasure is not his," Yamuna decided.

"Whose is it then?" Raghunath sounded annoyed.

Yamuna thought a bit. "You know what? He probably thinks he lost the pouch. If he thought he'd left it behind, he would have asked about it. That's good for us, don't you think? He doesn't suspect us, thank god," she said.

Raghunath said, "But he's seen all the improvements."

"So what. He can't prove anything."

It was getting late. There was a nip in the night air. Yamuna dozed off. But Raghunath could not sleep. He lay in bed, staring into the darkness.

What had Satyadas said? You are a good man …

Next morning, Raghunath woke up Satyadas. The peddler
packed his things and washed up. He was ready to leave, when
Raghunath said, "The sun isn't up yet. It's still misty outside. Why
don't you have a cup of tea? "

"Oh no babu, I can't. Give my regards to your lovely wife." He
wrapped the muffler about his head so that most of his face was
not visible. "Let me go, babu," he said, his hands coming together
in a namaskar.

Raghunath followed him outside. The morning mist had spread
over the fields. The grass was damp. Satyadas paused an instant.
Then he stepped out briskly.

Raghunath called out urgently. "Satyadas!"

He stopped.

Raghunath struggled with his thoughts. "Did you leave anything behind? The last time you came?" he blurted.

Satyadas turned. A strange smile crept to his lips. "Why do you ask, babu?"

"Did you?"

Satyadas looked up at the sky. "Only he can tell."

"He? You mean God?"

"The sun. He brings the day with him. Then comes night. Night and day – light and darkness. They have eyes, you know!"

Raghunath gasped. Two rings! The stones – one light, the other dark. Six coins!

Satyadas wiped the dew from his face. He seemed to know exactly what was going on in Raghunath's head.

"You know babu," he said. Day meets night in an eternal union. Six seasons dance around our earth in a never ending circle. Nothing escapes their notice – greed, sin, vice ... They watch over everything. Only we are unmindful of them. They see every lapse – every transgression. I am a poor illiterate man. It is not my place to speak of morals."

He bowed in a namaste. "I am sorry for you. I understand. Goodbye."

And Satyadas of Dharmapur melted into the mist.

Raghunath just stood there watching him go. It was as if he had turned to stone.

**Bimal Kar**: Born in Taki, North 24-Parganas, on 19 September 1921, Bimal Kar spent his early youth in Asansol and parts of Bihar. He was involved in myriad professions that later helped him write on varied subjects. His writings reflect a modern mind and have inspired many young writers whom he also supported at the start of their literary careers. For children, Kar created the retired magician Kinkar Kishore Ray, alias Kikira who solved mysteries with his two assistants. Kar also has to his credit several novels that were successfully adapted for the screen. These include the classic comedy, *Basanta-Bilap*, the evergreen *Balika Bodhu*, *Jadubangsha* and *Chhuti* (based on his novel, *Khar-Kuto*). From 1954 to 1982, he was associated with *Desh* where his novel *Grahan* was published in 1964. Asamay, also published in Desh, won him the Sahitya Akademi award in 1975. Kar won the Ananda Puraskar in 1967 and the Saratchandra Award from Calcutta University in 1981, among other honours.

**Neeta Gangopadhya**: A post graduate from the College of Art, New Delhi, Neeta Gangopadhya has illustrated several books for children. She has represented India at the Biennial of Illustrations, Bratislava in 1995. Her illustrations are included in the book Once Upon a Time in India, which has been nominated for the IBBY Honours List in 2006.

## About Katha

Katha, a nonprofit organization working with and in story and storytelling since 1988, is one of India's top publishing houses. Focussing on quality translations – our list includes more than 300 of India's best literary talents from 21 languages – we showcase contemporary Indian fiction like no other publisher. Katha also introduces an array of writings from the many oral and written traditions of India to children, ages 0 - 17.

Katha's major activities include the **Katha Awards for Literary Excellence** that are considered national recognitions; and the **Katha Festivals** and utsavs that bring literature into the public ken. These create open meeting places for writers, translators, scholars, critics, storytellers, folk and contemporary artists and community activists from India and abroad. Katha works with 6,000 Friends of Katha and a growing pool of writers, translators and literary enthusiasts.

Katha, with five international recognitions to its credit including the **NASDAQ STOCK MARKET EDUCATION AWARD** for 2002, is internationally known for its endeavours to spread the joy of reading, knowing, and living amongst adults and children, the common reader and the neo-literate. Story pedagogy® is an innovative classroom practice in Katha schools that work with communities in Delhi and other parts of India – helping more than 8,000 children and 250,000 adults across 72 communities bring positive change.

www.ingramcontent.com/pod-product-compliance
Lightning Source LLC
Chambersburg PA
CBHW081146170626
46809CB00011B/3167